A

DOGOPOTAMUS
The Most Awesomest Pet Ever. Maybe.

Michael Andrew Fox
Illustrated by Ed Shems

PETIMALS ®
DOGOPOTAMUS ™   SECOND EDITION

For more information, visit us online at:
www.petimalsbooks.com

Like us on Facebook at:
www.facebook.com/petimals

A PETIMALS Book

DOGOPOTAMUS
The Most Awesomest Pet Ever. Maybe.

Michael Andrew Fox
Illustrated by Ed Shems

FOR ZACK AND COBY.

CONTENTS

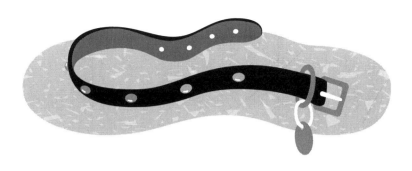

1
THE BIG DAY

I dashed downstairs, just like I did every

morning, and sat at the breakfast table. I was

nervous, but confident. Today was the day. I

had just one shot, and this was it. I had waited long enough, rehearsed the lines in my head, over and over and over.

I could feel my blue pajama pants dangling just above my ankles. None of my pajama pants actually make it to the ground. I must grow when I'm sleeping, or maybe they shrink overnight. Why is that? Wait, I can't worry about that now, I need to focus! I had more important things on my mind. It was time…to ask for a pet.

But, not just any pet. Anybody could ask for a cat or a fish or a guinea pig. My boring older brother Zack had turtles. Lame! You can't walk a turtle, they're not fun to pet, and if you so much as sneeze, they disappear into their shell. What fun is that? I want something better. Something bigger! The most awesomest pet EVER!

It wasn't going to be easy. Mom was whirling around the kitchen making breakfast, fixing lunches; doing first-thing-in-the-morning stuff. Cereal again? Who decided cereal was the number one breakfast food in the world, by the way? Ugh! Focus!

Mom made a second spin past the breakfast table and I went for it.

"Mom" I said, a bit of chocolate cereal still caught in the back of my throat. "Can I have my own pet?"

"What honey?" She said as she raced out of the kitchen and into the laundry room.

I knew morning was my best shot because Dad had already left for work. If I waited until dinner, I would have to deal with both of them. That wasn't going to work. If I could get my Mom to sit still for two seconds, I'd have her one-on-one. Mornings are full of distractions, and she might not be awake enough to realize she said yes to my request. You might not know it, but according to the kid / parent contract, a verbal yes is binding as far as I'm concerned. Here she comes again.

"Mom, I asked if I could have my own pet."

I didn't think she heard me, but just as she was about to leave the room, she stopped short and quickly turned around.

"Coby, you want a pet? Like your brother?"

Yeah right! What would I do with turtles? Ever try to make a turtle fetch? I might as well ask for a pet rock.

"Not exactly, Mom," I said, with as much sincerity as I could muster. "I would like something bigger. It would be the best pet ever! And I would have the only one."

Her hands were on her hips, her head tilted slightly to the side. She raised one eyebrow and asked, "What exactly did you have in mind?"

Even Zack, who doesn't pay attention to anything in the morning, stopped stuffing his face and looked up from across the table. I took a deep breath and swallowed. They both stared at me, waiting for my answer. Here goes nothing.

"I would like to have…as a pet…my very own …hippopotamus."

The word just hung there, like an echo in a deep, dark cave. I could hear my own heartbeat and time seemed to stop. Nobody moved or even breathed for what seemed like an eternity.

Mom turned to Zack, Zack stared at me, I looked at my Mom, and somewhere in the house two North American Box Turtles quickly retreated into their shells.

"Coby, you CANNOT have a hippopotamus," my Mom finally said, breaking the silence.

"That's the dumbest thing I've ever heard, Coby," my brother added, shaking his head while shoveling in more cereal.

"Why can't I have a hippo?"

Here comes my pitch. I was ready for this.

"I'll take good care of him. We can dig a hole in the backyard and fill it with water. How cool would that be to have a hippo in the back yard? I can take him for walks. I've seen the ones at the zoo, they don't move around that much. It would be awesome!"

I rushed it a bit, but I got out the important points. She would have to at least consider it, right?

"There is NO way you can have a hippopotamus," she said. "First of all, they're NOT pets. Second, you can't just go to a pet store and buy a hippo. Third, they're too big to keep in the house. And, most importantly, I'm sure it's not allowed by our homeowners association."

Rats! I had anticipated most of these arguments and thought I had a comeback for them all. But I didn't see that last one coming.

Good one, Mom. I'd rather fight City Hall than go up against the Belleview Acres Homeowners Association. This might be a problem.

"How about a dog?" she asked, as she sped down the hallway and up the stairs.

"But everyone's got a dog," I mumbled, slumping back in the chair. "I want something different."

I put my head down. Mom was gone again, continuing to race between the kitchen, living room and laundry room. Zack was giggling to himself and muttering something about hippos making stupid pets. I could only sit there and wonder if my hippo hopes were squashed forever.

2

IT'S A CRUEL WORLD

The pet subject didn't come up at dinner, so I just let it go for now. That night, as I lay in bed, I could only think about the cruel, unfair world in which I was living. Who decides what's a pet and what isn't? A dog has four legs. So does a hippo. A dog has two eyes, two ears, lots of teeth, and a tail. So do hippos. Dogs like to eat, swim, and lay in the grass. Hippo! Hippo! Hippo! Granted, hippos tend to be slightly larger than dogs, but who says dogs make good pets and hippos don't?

The wheels in my head started turning. What if I could take all the things I love about hippos, and combine that with all the things I like about dogs. Wouldn't that be the ultimate pet? Hmmm...

This could be the answer. The perfect solution to my pet problem. I might have found a loophole. I sat down at my desk, dug out some paper from the bottom drawer, and

took out a blue Crayola.

I drew a head, body, four legs, and a tail. I like floppy ears, so let's add those, but the head and mouth need to be big like a hippo.

I kept drawing, and I could see what was in my head starting to take shape on the paper.

Keep the dog's nose and add a tongue for licking. Let's make the body big, smooth and shiny, no fur.

More and more I saw my creation forming

in front of my eyes.

Hippos have lame tails, so we'll keep the

dog's. I drew a nice long tail so he can wag it

when he sees me. The crayon moved faster and faster. Add a couple of wrinkles here, bulge out the eyes a bit there, fix the toes, add some teeth and there you have it!

20

I pushed away from the desk and leaned back in the chair to soak in what I had created. It could only be described as a work of art – the Mona Lisa of the animal kingdom! Behold, the very first of its kind! The one, the only….Dogopotamus!

It was perfect. I grabbed 4 pushpins and carefully hung my creation above my bed. I lay down, hands behind my head and with a smile from ear to ear I stared at my new best friend. I could picture the possibilities…

3

DOGO ROCKS

I imagined taking Dogopotamus for walks through the neighborhood. Everyone would stop and watch as we walked.

"Hi, Mrs. Cordell," I would say as we strolled by.

"Good morning, Coby. How is Dogopotamus today?"

"He's good. Just out for our morning walk."

As we moved through the streets, Dogopotamus would stop and smell something, take a break, and then keep walking. He was fun to walk. Not too fast, not too slow. Just sniffing around with that great, big nose and wagging that wonderful tail.

We lived in a nice area with sidewalks, big trees, and lots of space. Nothing seemed to bother Dogopotamus. We walked by the park, and all the kids came running over to check out my new best friend.

"Coby, that's the coolest pet I've ever seen," said my neighbor, Brent. "What is it?"

"It's a Dogopotamus," I said, with tons of pride in my voice.

I could hear all the kids talking about him and wishing they had one of their own. I was instantly the coolest kid in the neighborhood. They would slowly reach out and pet him, and marvel at how big he was. Dogopotamus was gentle and calm, and just stood there while everyone surrounded him.

Eventually it was time to leave and all the kids slowly walked back to the playground, looking back over their shoulders, still in awe of the creature they had just seen. As Dogopotamus and I started to walk away, I could tell my legs were a little tired.

He must have noticed as well, and lowered his front legs in front of me as if to say, "Climb aboard".

"Really? I can actually ride you?"

I stepped up on his front left leg, grabbed his big head, and threw my right leg over his huge back. I scooted myself up onto his neck, grabbed his ears, and he stood up nice and slow so he wouldn't knock me off. He started to walk and as we made our way down the street, I would tug on each ear to direct him. If I pulled a little on the right ear, we'd go right, and same for the left. I was steering him just like a car.

With every giant step he took, I would sway side to side. The ride was a little bouncy, but I loved it. Once we got home, he lowered me down and I hopped off.

"Thanks for the ride, Dogopotamus," I said with a huge smile on my face.

I opened the back gate to the house and he found the hole we had dug for him in the backyard that was filled with muddy water. He lowered himself in and I could tell he was relaxed and happy. Having Dogopotamus for a pet is SO awesome!

4

SILLY SQUIRREL

The next day, I got up and walked out to the

back yard to see Dogopotamus. He was

already standing by the back gate, and I could

tell he was excited to go for another walk. I

opened the back gate and off we went. This

time, we strolled past the park and just walked in a circle around the neighborhood.

As usual, everyone in the neighborhood stopped as we walked by. We reached the corner, just up the street from our house and Dogopotamus needed a break. We stopped and he sat down beside me to catch his breath. Just as we were about to get going again, Dogopotamus noticed something moving a few feet away from us. I looked to see what he was looking at. It was a harmless squirrel.

Staring back at us, it locked eyes with my new, overweight pet. The squirrel decided it didn't want to mess with my 4000-pound friend and headed for the nearest tree. Before I could even blink, Dogopotamus took off!

Like a freight train, he was rumbling across the lawns, kicking up grass and nearly yanking my arms out of their sockets as I struggled to hang on.

The squirrel managed to dart up a tree, but Dogopotamus didn't stop. He lowered his head and ran into that tree as if it wasn't even there. The tree came tumbling down half in the yard and half in the street. He spotted the squirrel again as it scurried across the street, and Dogopotamus was right on its tail. Who knew something this big could move so fast? As he plowed across the street, I looked back and saw huge paw prints in the pavement. Dogopotamus was leaving giant potholes everywhere he went. Trees and telephone poles were falling all over the neighborhood. The squirrel would run up a tree, Dogopotamus would knock it down, and the squirrel would search for another. The neighborhood was starting to look as if a tornado had hit it.

Finally, the squirrel managed to get away, or Dogopotamus just decided to take a break.

He sat down beside me, catching his breath. I felt like I had taken a roller coaster ride through our neighborhood.

"Let's go Dogopotamus, we better get home."

He finally got up, turned around and we slowly headed back towards our house, weaving in and out of fallen trees, and severed branches that were scattered all over the street. Potholes in the shape of Hippo feet covered the lawns and pavement. He came up beside me, gave me a little nudge on the leg and looked up at me with those big, sad, bulging eyes. For a split second, I thought maybe he was sorry for what he had done, but I'm pretty sure he was just upset he never got that squirrel.

5

FeTCH?

We get back to our house, I open the gate and put Dogopotamus in the backyard. He finds his swimming hole and waddles over to it. Sticking his mouth under the surface, he takes a big drink and then slowly submerges himself as the sides overflow with muddy water. Even though all I can see is his eyes, nose and ears sticking up, I know he has a smile on his face again.

I decide to let Dogopotamus enjoy his swim and I go inside. I sit down on the couch in the living room, exhausted. Walking Dogopotamus didn't go exactly how I had hoped. But that was just one setback. I thought about what else Dogopotamus would like to do. What about a game of fetch? Dogs love to play fetch. That should be fun. And, we can do that in the backyard. I walk out to the garage to start looking around. We have one of those big, blue plastic buckets that we keep all the balls in. I dig around in the corner behind the trashcans and find the bucket.

It's filled to the top with toys, sports equipment and tons of different kinds of balls. Rubber balls, tennis balls, volleyballs, baseballs, footballs. You name the ball, we got it. I even see a beach ball in there.

Unfortunately, tennis balls always seem to fall to the very bottom. I reach my hand in and start working my way down. I finally pull out an old, faded green tennis ball.

I walk out back and find Dogopotamus still soaking in his hole. He sees me, slowly crawls out and comes over. I show him the tennis ball and he immediately perks up.

"You want to play fetch, boy?" I ask.

Dogopotamus starts wagging his tail and his whole body shakes.

I take the tennis ball and toss it to the other side of the yard. He spins around and takes off. The ground rumbles as he dashes across the lawn. I see him pick up the tennis ball and he runs back towards me. He stops right in front of me and sits down. His tongue is hanging out and he's just looking at me.

"Drop it," I say.

Dogopotamus just looks at me, panting.

"You need to drop it so I can throw it again," I say, still waiting.

Dogopotamus just sits there, staring back at me. Finally, he yawns a big yawn and I look inside his huge mouth. No tennis ball! What happened to it? I saw him pick it up. Did he eat it?

I run into the garage dig my hand into the bucket again and find another one. I go back outside and find Dogopotamus sitting in the same spot waiting.

"Here you go buddy. Bring it back this time," I say as I chuck the ball across the backyard.

Dogopotamus takes off again, picks up the ball and lumbers back towards me. He sits down and stares at me again. No ball.

I think he's eating them instead of fetching them!

Maybe tennis balls are too small. I run back to the garage, find a volleyball and bring that back.

"Let's try this, boy." I say.

The volleyball is light, but still too big for me to throw with just one hand. I grab it with both hands and toss it. Not as far as the tennis ball, but still far enough. Dogopotamus turns and takes off after it. He picks it up in his enormous mouth, turns and comes back to me. He sits down and stares at me.

"You got to be kidding me!" I say. "You ate that one too?"

Back to the garage I go and grab a basketball. The basketball is a bit bigger than the volleyball and a little heavier.

I stand in front of Dogopotamus again, grab the basketball with both hands, swing my arms from side to side to get some momentum and chuck it as far as I can. Dogopotamus follows the ball with his eyes as it flies over his head, then he runs after it. He picks it up, comes back and sits down. No ball.

"Wow, this is crazy." I say out loud.

I go back to the garage and look inside the blue bucket. The only ball bigger than the basketball is the beach ball. It's the kind you blow up with your mouth.

It is mostly white, but it has red, yellow and blue colored stripes. It doesn't weigh much, so I'm not sure how far I can actually throw it. I walk back and stand in front of Dogopotamus one more time.

"Fetch it. Don't eat it. Ok?" I ask.

He just looks back at me with those big eyes, tail wagging and tongue still hanging out.

"Don't eat it. Not food." I say, hoping he understands, but knowing he has no idea what I'm saying.

I decide to dropkick the ball across the yard to get more distance. It flies across the yard, spinning all of its colors in the air.

Dogopotamus runs after it, and as soon as he puts his mouth on it I hear a loud pop. He turns around and comes back towards me with pieces of beach ball shreds hanging from his teeth. It obviously exploded all over his mouth like a bubble gum bubble. He sits down in front of me, bits of plastic hanging from his mouth and teeth.

"Well, I'm not sure what to do now, buddy." I say, scratching my head.

Wait a minute! If he's eating all the balls, then I know what's going on...he's hungry!

6

BOTTOMLESS PIT

I looked at my watch and it was lunchtime.
I didn't realize it, but I was hungry too…and
a little dizzy from being dragged around the
neighborhood and running back and forth to
the garage.

I went inside and found Mom in the kitchen.

"Mom, can I have some lunch please?" I asked.

"Sure, Coby." My Mom said with a cheery voice. "But you better feed Dogopotamus first."

I looked out the window, and there he was, waiting by the door. Tail wagging and mouth open wide. Even though he just ate 2 tennis balls, a volleyball, a basketball and a beach ball, I guess he should probably eat some real food. I went to the fridge and grabbed some lettuce, carrots and other veggies that we bought just for him. I opened the door and he was excited. I have to remember not to play fetch with him before lunch next time.

"Let's do this on the back porch so we don't make a mess in the kitchen," I said, as I grabbed a chair to stand on.

The tail wagged faster and his mouth opened wider. I took a whole carrot and threw it right in his mouth. It disappeared into the darkness. He closed his mouth for a second, tilted his head back, opened his mouth again and was ready for more. I grabbed an entire package of iceberg lettuce, unwrapped it, and threw it in. This time, Dogopotamus didn't even flinch. Mouth still open, tail still wagging. I took the rest of the carrots, 10 of them, and threw them in one by one. He didn't seem to chew. He just tilted his head back for a second and waited for more.

I grabbed some cucumbers, bell peppers, another package of lettuce and everything else we had in the veggie drawer from the fridge. I just threw everything in. I went to the fruit drawer and grabbed the apples, oranges, melons, and bananas. I dumped them all in. He just looked at me for a split second, smiled, and opened his mouth again.

More? You gotta be kidding me!

I thought about what else I could feed him, and then I had an idea. Since Dogopotamus was half dog, he'd probably like dog food. I ran next door to the Cordell's house. They had a little schnauzer named Tramp. I went into the garage and dragged a 25-pound bag of kibble across the lawn, through the gate, and onto the back porch. I grabbed a frying pan from the kitchen and started shoveling.

Scoop after scoop, he would chew, swallow,

and then ask for more. Finally, I was down to

the last bit, so I picked up the bag and

dumped the rest into his enormous mouth. He

chewed, he swallowed, and then he opened

his mouth again. Now I was getting worried.

This is just one meal!

I ran over to the cupboard, and took

everything out. Bread, cereal, granola bars,

chips, fruit snacks, crackers. You name it; I

grabbed it and threw it into the bottomless pit.

I opened every drawer, and emptied every

shelf. Finally, when all the cupboards were bare, and every ounce of food was gone from the house, Dogopotamus was done. He slowly wandered back to his watering hole, gave a big yawn and sank back into the mud pit. I sat down at the table and looked at the kitchen. Empty boxes, and torn packages were scattered all over the floor. He had eaten everything we had.

Maybe Dogopotamus was going to be harder than I thought.

7

DOGO DESTRUCTION

Later, I was brushing my teeth, washing my face and getting ready for bed when I heard a noise by the back door. I walked downstairs, and there was Dogopotamus, rubbing his nose on the back door window. He was wagging his tail and waiting for something.

I wasn't sure I wanted to open the door just yet, so I said through the glass, "What's up, buddy? What are you waiting for?"

He nudged the door again with his nose and I realized what he wanted. He wanted to come in. I guess it would be okay. If I had a dog, it would sleep in my room at the foot of my bed. Why not a Dogopotamus?

"Okay boy, come on in. Gently please."

I opened the door, and Dogopotamus walked slowly inside. He got halfway through the door and stopped. I had no idea why.

"Come on, Dogopotamus. It's okay." I reassured.

I couldn't tell if he was nervous, afraid or what. He started to take another step, but couldn't. Then I realized what was going on. He was stuck. I hadn't anticipated this little problem. He was only slightly larger then the doorway, close enough that I thought I could probably help him squeeze through from the other side. I went out the front, and came around to the back through the gate.

The tail had stopped wagging at this point, and I could tell that Dogopotamus was probably getting a little scared.

"Don't worry, buddy. I can help."

I leaned my shoulder into his backside and pushed as hard as I could. Dogopotamus started shuffling his feet and wiggling side to side. Inch by inch, he started moving forward. I started to hear cracking and creaking coming from the door frame, and just as I started to think this was a bad idea, there was a loud pop as the door frame split on one side and the door itself flew off the hinges and landed on the kitchen floor. Dogopotamus and I both fell into the house with a loud crash and the kitchen table toppled over.

"I hope Mom didn't hear that." I said.

Once inside, he was excited to check out all the new sights and smells and started making his way around the first floor of the house. He squeezed his way down the hallway, barely fitting and managed to wipe everything off the walls; artwork, picture frames, even my Mom's antique clock. Everything came crashing down behind him. I also noticed that everywhere he went, he left perfect

Dogopotamus footprints dented into the hardwood floor.

"What's going on down there?" Mom yelled from upstairs. "I thought I heard a crash."

You heard a crash all right. That was the sound of my hippopotamus dreams being shattered with every dent in the hardwood and every broken picture frame on the floor. Dogopotamus made his way to the bottom of the staircase and took a good long look up the stairs. Then he looked over at me and all I could do was shake my head.

"Don't even try it," I said out loud, even though I knew he was going to anyway.

He put his right foot up on the first step, just to test it out. It seemed to hold, so he shifted his weight and pulled the left foot up to the second step. As soon as all of his weight shifted over to the left foot, I heard a groan coming from the staircase. He took his right foot, planted it on the third step, and lifted his back right leg up onto the first step behind him.

The groan quickly turned into a series of cracks and pops, and the staircase began to sway and shake.

Dogopotamus kept going as the staircase trembled beneath him, and with one large explosive snap, the staircase gave in to the 4000 pounds that was standing on it. We both watched as the staircase came crashing down around us.

As the dust swirled around me, all I could think about were the trees and branches littered all across the neighborhood. The overflowing mud pit in the backyard. Empty boxes, bare cupboards and blank shelves in the kitchen. Busted doorways, broken picture frames, dented floors and a shattered staircase.

What would Mom say? What would the neighbors say? What would the Belleview Acres Homeowners Association say?

8

PHEW

Fighting back tears, I closed my eyes hoping everything would just go away. At that very moment, the noise was gone. The smell of torn wood and drywall dust were no longer there. I slowly opened my eyes and as they began to focus, I realized where I was. It was the next morning, I was lying in bed, and there in front of me, held up by 4 simple pushpins, was Dogopotamus, just as I had drawn him. What a nightmare!

I got up and headed downstairs. I came to the top of the staircase and stopped. I could only smile as I took each step on my way down to the hallway. Picture frames intact, artwork still hung and the antique clock still ticking away. I made my way across the shiny hardwood floor and sat at my usual spot at the breakfast table, which was right where it was the day before. The cupboards were full, the fridge was stocked and my pajama pants were still dangling just above my ankles. And, my brother Zack was still stuffing his face with fruity cereal.

Mom was whirling around as usual but stopped when she saw me.

"Good morning Coby," she said. "You don't still want a hippo as a pet, do you?"

"Nope," I said. "I think I can come up with something better."

With hands on her hips, and her head tilted slightly to the side, she raised one eyebrow and turned towards Zack, whose spoon froze halfway between the bowl and his face.

Mom looked at Zack, Zack looked at me, I looked at my Mom, and somewhere in the house two North American Box Turtles quickly retreated into their shells.

THE END

Here's a preview of the next Petimals Book,

HAMSTIGATOR

Available Now!

The first rays of morning sunlight come through my bedroom window. I watch a beam of yellow slowly creep across the wall next to my bed. I've been awake for a while, staring at the ceiling, just waiting to get up and go downstairs for breakfast. The breakfast table is where I do my best work. It's my office. My sharpest negotiating tactics all take place between the hours of 6:30 and 7:45 a.m. Instead of fancy chairs, coffee, and three-piece suits, my boardroom consists of a round, wood table, fruity cereal, and sharky pajamas. Shirt optional.

My target: adults over the age of 30 who, somehow in their advanced age, have lost the ability to think clearly before 7 o'clock. Perfect situation for me. Anytime I want something, need something, or have to bargain for something, this is THE time to do it. Unfortunately, my biggest roadblock is my older brother, Zack. Nobody kills a perfectly executed plan like he does. He's equal parts boring, lame, and annoying. Zack thinks all my ideas are stupid, and instead of just sitting there minding his own business, he has to make a face or a comment, or otherwise say something that somehow snaps our groggy parents out of their morning fog. No breakfast table board meeting ever goes well when he's around.

That's why I've been staring at the ceiling above my bed for the past hour. Today's negotiation is particularly important. I'm ready, again, to ask for a pet. I'm not talking about just any pet. This one is going to be special, and it will require special bargaining tactics. I need total concentration and no distractions. Dad isn't around this morning because he's traveling for work. Zack should still be asleep, so it'll just be Mom and me. Mano a Momo.

I get up and put a matching pajama shirt on today. You're always taken more seriously with a shirt on. Even though it's nearly summer and I don't sleep with one when it gets hot, I feel like I should be slightly more formal this morning. I could put on slippers, or actually get dressed for school, but that would be a dead giveaway that I was up to something. I open my door as quietly as I can and slowly walk down the hallway towards the stairs.

There is no way to get downstairs without having to pass by my brother's room. What a pain! The floors are made of hardwood, and it seems each step I take creates a symphony of cracks and pops. What's up with floors not making noise any other time of the day, but early in the morning they sound like I'm stepping on bubble wrap? I hate hardwood floors!

As quietly as I can, I make my way past Zack's door. As I sneak by, I hear the faintest sound of scurrying. One of Zack's turtles, I'm sure. Not exactly the greatest lookout pet. Lame.

I head downstairs, slowly making my way through the first floor hallway and into the kitchen. I sit at the table and wait. The old clock on the wall reads 6:15 a.m. A little early, but any minute now Mom will come into the kitchen and my workday will begin.

It seems like an eternity. I swear I can hear that old clock on the wall tick-tick-ticking away. Finally, at 6:25 a.m. Mom emerges from her bedroom. With her eyes half-closed, she stumbles into the kitchen. I adjust myself in the chair and scoot in a little closer to the table, trying to make it look like I had just sat down.

"Morning Coby," Mom says, wiping her eyes with the back of her hands. "You're up early today."

"Morning Mom. Yeah, I just got up."
Wink, wink.

She stretches out her arms, and in the middle of a yawn says, "A-a-a-r-e y-y-o-o-u r-e-e-a-a-dy for breakfast? I can make you some cereal."

Perfect! She's barely awake.

"Sure," I say, rolling my eyes. Cereal again? Seriously? Is there nothing else in this house for breakfast?

Mom moves in slow motion as she tries to locate all the super complicated ingredients that make up a bowl of cereal. She goes from the pantry to the fridge, back to the pantry, over to the cupboard, back to the fridge, pulls out 3 drawers before she finds a spoon, back to the pantry and finally over to the kitchen table. It's like watching a Ping-Pong game at half speed.

I'm pretty sure she put the milk back in the cupboard and the box of cereal back in the fridge. This is going to be easier than I thought.

She sits down at the table to catch her breath. I take one spoonful of sugary cereal for a burst of energy and decide there's no time like the present. Here goes nothing...

"Mom, I would REALLY like to have my own pet," I say, easing her into the conversation.

"What exactly did you have in mind this time, Coby?" she asks as another yawn comes out.

This time? Obviously she hasn't forgotten about last time. Dogopotamus was a great idea on paper, but he was just too big. I need something cool, but compact. The perfect combination of exciting and fun, but medium-sized and manageable. And, I think I've found it!

"I have the perfect idea, Mom," I say as I sit up in my chair and lean forward into my pitch position.

I didn't think you could stop a yawn midway through, but Mom seems to manage it. She furrows her eyebrows, squints at me in the morning light and waits.

"Mom…I would like to have…as my very own pet…a medium sized…alligator."

The word "Alligator" just hangs there between us like a thought bubble in comic strips. I can hear my own heartbeat as the whole house goes silent. Even the clock on the wall stops ticking.

Mom stares at me, I stare at Mom, Zack rolls over in bed, and somewhere in the house one of the North American Box Turtles flips over onto its shell.

ABOUT THE AUTHOR

Michael Andrew Fox is an Emmy Award winning television producer and author. Inspired by his own 2 boys, Michael rekindled his passion for writing with his NEW children's book series, Petimals. Dogopotamus is his first book.

Michael lives in Littleton, Colorado with his wife Eileen and 2 boys, Zack and Coby.

Visit his website: **www.petimalsbooks.com**

ABOUT THE ILLUSTRATOR

Ed Shems has been illustrating and designing since 1991. Since graduating from the Rhode Island School of Design, Ed has illustrated more than 25 children's books and is currently writing and illustrating his own stories.

Visit his website: **www.edfredned.com**

Made in the USA
San Bernardino, CA
08 September 2014